Puppy Mudge
Wants to Play

By Cynthia Rylant

Illustrated by Suçie Stevenson

READY-TO-READ

SIMON & SCHUSTER BOOKS FOR YOUNG READERS
New York   London   Toronto   Sydney

SIMON & SCHUSTER BOOKS FOR YOUNG READERS
An imprint of Simon & Schuster Children's Publishing Division
1230 Avenue of the Americas, New York, New York 10020
Text copyright © 2005 by Cynthia Rylant
Illustrations copyright © 2005 by Suçie Stevenson
SIMON & SCHUSTER BOOKS FOR YOUNG READERS is a trademark of Simon & Schuster, Inc.
READY-TO-READ is a registered trademark of Simon & Schuster, Inc.
Book design by Daniel Roode
The text for this book is set in Goudy.
The illustrations for this book are rendered in pen-and-ink and watercolor.
Manufactured in the United States of America
10 9 8 7 6 5 4 3
CIP data for this book is available from the Library of Congress.
ISBN 0-689-83984-7

This is Henry's puppy, Mudge.
Mudge wants to play.

Henry is reading.
Henry does not want to play.

Mudge cannot read.

Mudge wants to play.

Mudge pulls off Henry's sock.

"Aw, Mudge," says Henry.

Henry reads.

Mudge chews up Henry's laces.

"Aw, Mudge," says Henry.

Henry reads.
Mudge sits on Henry's foot.

Mudge sits on Henry's lap.

Mudge sits on Henry's book.
Mudge looks at Henry.

Mudge looks and looks and
looks at Henry.
"Mudge," asks Henry, "do you
want to play?"

Mudge jumps.
Mudge dances.

Mudge goes round and round.

Mudge WANTS TO PLAY.

So they do!